VITA BREVIS

A Letter to St Augustine

JOSTEIN GAARDER

Illustrated by
SARAH PERKINS

Translated by
ANNE BORN

PHŒNIX

A Phoenix Paperback
First published in Great Britain by Phoenix House in 1997
This paperback edition published in 1998 by Phoenix,
a division of Orion Books Ltd,
Orion House, 5 Upper St Martin's Lane,
London WC2H 9EA

A CIP catalogue record for this book
is available from the British Library.

ISBN: 0 75380 125 6

Typeset by Deltatype Ltd, Birkenhead, Merseyside
Printed and bound in Great Britain by
Clays Ltd, St Ives plc

The critics on Jostein Gaarder's
international bestseller
SOPHIE'S WORLD

'A marvellously rich book. Its success boils down to
something quite simple – Gaarder's gift for communi-
cating ideas'   *Guardian*

'An Alice in Wonderland for the 90s . . . already
Sophie's World is being talked up as philosophy's
answer to Stephen Hawking's *A Brief History of Time*
. . . this is a simply wonderful, irresistible book'
                                        Daily Telegraph

'Remarkable . . . what Jostein Gaarder has managed
to do is condense 3000 years of thought into 400 pages;
to simplify some extremely complicated arguments
without trivialising them . . . *Sophie's World* is an
extraordinary achievement'   *Sunday Times*

'Challenging, informative and packed with easily
grasped, and imitable, ways of thinking about difficult
ideas'   *Independent on Sunday*

'*Sophie's World* is a whimsical and ingenious mystery
novel that also happens to be a history of philosophy
. . . What is admirable in the novel is the utter unpre-
tentiousness of the philosophical lessons . . . which
manages to deliver Western philosophy in accounts
that are crystal clear'   *Washington Post*

'A terrifically entertaining and imaginative story
wrapped round its tough, thought-provoking philosophical heart'   *Daily Mail*

'Seductive and original . . . *Sophie's World* is, as it
dares to congratulate itself, "a strange and wonderful
book"'   *TLS*

Jostein Gaarder was born in Oslo in 1952. *Sophie's World*, the first of his books to be published in English, has been published in 40 languages and has been a bestseller in each of them.

BY THE SAME AUTHOR

Sophie's World
The Solitaire Mystery
The Christmas Mystery
Hello? Is Anybody There?

W HEN I VISITED *the book fair in Buenos Aires in the spring of 1995 I was urged to set aside a morning for the renowned flea market in San Telmo. After a few hectic hours in front of all the stalls on streets and market-places I ended up taking refuge in a small antiquarian bookshop. Among a modest selection of old manuscripts my eyes were drawn to a red box file labelled 'Codex Floriae.' Something must have aroused my interest, for I opened the box carefully and looked down at a bundle of handwritten sheets. They were certainly old, extremely old, and moreover I quickly realised that the text was in Latin.*

An introductory greeting was written in large letters on a single line: 'Floria Aemilia Aurelio Augustino Episcopo Hipponiensi Salutem.' Greetings from Floria Aemilia to Aurelius Augustine, Bishop of Hippo ... So it must be a letter. But could it really be written to the theologian and church father who spent most of his life in North Africa from the middle of the fourth century onwards? From someone who called herself Floria?

I was already well acquainted with Augustine's biography. No other single figure shows more clearly the dramatic change of culture through the transition from the old Greco-Roman to the universal Christian culture which was to characterise Europe right up to our own time. The best source of Augustine's life is naturally Augustine himself. Through his Confessions

3

(Confessiones, *c. 400 AD*) he provides a unique insight into both the turbulent fourth century in general and into his own spiritual conflicts relating to faith and doubt. Augustine is probably the pre-Renaissance individual who is closest to ourselves.

Who was the woman who could have written a long letter to him? For the box held at least 70 or 80 sheets. I had never heard of any such document.

I tried to translate another sentence. 'As a matter of fact, it seems odd to address you in this way. Once, long, long ago, I would merely have written to "My playful little Aurel."' I couldn't be quite certain about the translation, but that the letter was in a highly personal tone I was left in no doubt.

Then something struck me. Could the letter in the red box file possibly be from Augustine's concubine of many years' standing, and therefore from the woman he had had to renounce, as he himself writes, because he had elected to spend the rest of his life abstaining from all sensual love? A shudder ran down my back, for I knew well that the Augustinian tradition knows no more either about the unfortunate woman or about her many years of cohabiting with Augustine other than the account of it he himself gives in the Confessions.

Soon the proprietor of the bookshop was beside me; he pointed down at the box file. I was still spellbound by the significance of the manuscript I had been trying to assess.

'Really something,' he said.

'Yes, I guess so ...'

There had already been some interviews with me in newspapers and on television in connection with the book fair, and now he recognised me:

'El Mundo de Sofía?'

4

I nodded, then he bent over the box, closed it and placed it tidily on top of a small pile of other manuscripts, as if to emphasise that he was not exactly burning to sell this one. Maybe he was slightly more doubtful since he now knew who I was.

'A letter to Saint Augustine?' I asked.

I thought he smiled uneasily.

'And you believe it's genuine?'

He said:

'It's not impossible. But I've only had it for a few hours, and if I'd known that this document is what it purports to be it wouldn't be lying here.'

'How did you get hold of it?'

He laughed:

'I wouldn't have lasted in this line very long if I hadn't learned to protect my clients.'

I was beginning to feel on tenterhooks. I asked:

'How much are you asking for it?'

'Fifteen thousand pesos.'

Fifteen thousand, that was like a punch in the side. For a manuscript that could certainly be several hundred years old, but which professed to be a letter from Augustine's concubine. At best we could be talking about a transcript of a hitherto unknown letter to the church father, or more likely a copy of an even older transcript.

Well, naturally it could just as well have been written in a Latin-American monastery some time during the seventeenth or eighteenth century. True enough, even that could be quite something to take back to Europe. I thought I'd heard that in certain religious communities this kind of apocryphal letter was written to or from Catholic saints now and again.

He began to shut up shop, and I passed him my Visa card.

'Twelve thousand pesos,' I said.

It was almost a hundred thousand kroner – for something that might not have any antiquarian value whatsoever. But I was curious, and I wasn't the first person to pay dear for his curiosity. Even when I first read Augustine's Confessions many years earlier I had tried to put myself in the place of this concubine. And Augustine's view of the love between man and woman has left extraordinarily clear traces behind it.

The bookseller accepted the offer. He said:

'I think we'd be wisest to regard this transaction as a kind of risk-spreading.'

I shook my head, for I couldn't grasp what he meant. Then he explained:

'Either I'm making an extremely good bargain or you're making an even better one.'

He printed off the details of my card and said sorrowfully:

'I haven't even managed to read the manuscript myself. In a few days the price would either have doubled or I would have chucked the box into that basket you see over there.'

I cast a glance at the basket he indicated; it was full of old paperbacks. On a sticker fixed to the basket I read: '2 pesos.'

It was I who had the best of the bargain. The 'Codex Floriae' has now been dated to the end of the sixteenth century, and was most probably penned in Argentina. The big question is merely whether an old parchment from which the 'Codex Floriae' was transcribed really did exist.

I myself am no longer in any doubt about the authenticity of the letter, and about whether in fact it must be attributed to Augustine's lover of many years. I feel it is almost impossible to imagine that it could have been fabricated in Argentina towards the end of the sixteenth century. So in spite of everything, it is simpler to assume that it really does originate from Augustine's time. Both the syntax and vocabulary of the manuscript are as if carved out of late antiquity, as also is Floria's blend of sensuality and an almost desperate religious reflection.

In the autumn of 1995 I took the manuscript to the Vatican Library in Rome for a more accurate analysis. But I was given scant help there. On the contrary: the Vatican maintained persistently that they have never received any 'Codex Floriae'. That doesn't surprise me, although I can't just out of hand accept that Floria's letter belongs to the Catholic Church.

I had naturally taken care to make a photocopy of the manuscript, and during the spring of 1996 I attempted to garb the letter in Norwegian dress. Where the letter cites Augustine's Confessions, *though, I chose to resort to Oddmund Hjelde's outstanding Norwegian translation of the first ten books.*

The work of translation has been a jigsaw puzzle without parallel, not least because the manuscript has no pagination. At the same time it has been immensely stimulating to have this opportunity to brush up on my old facility in Latin – acquired long ago at Oslo Cathedral School (1968–71). Many a time I had to send a grateful thought to my old Latin teacher, Oskar Fjeld.

It is fascinating how old conjugations and declinations remain as if nailed to the memory. Nevertheless, without the benevolent assistance of Øivind Andersen this translation would not have been possible. Thanks also for encouraging words and good advice to Trond Berg Eriksen, Egil Kraggerud, Øyvind Norderval and Kari Vogt.

Nothing would please me more than if this edition of the 'Codex Floriae' should be rewarded by a renewal of interest in the Latin language and in classical culture as a whole.

I

1   i.e. listener. Floria uses the Latin word *auditor*.

GREETINGS FROM
FLORIA AEMILIA,
TO AURELIUS AUGUSTINE,
BISHOP OF HIPPO.

As A MATTER of fact it seems odd to address you in this way. Once, long, long ago, I would merely have written to 'My playful little Aurel.' But now more than ten years have passed since you put your arms around me, and much has changed.

I write because the priest of Carthage has allowed me to read your confessions. He thought your books might be edifying reading for a woman like me. As a catechumen[1] I've belonged in a way to the congregation here for many years already, but I shall not allow myself to be baptised, Aurel. It is not the Nazarene who stands in my way, neither is it the four gospels, but I shall not be baptised.

In Book Six you write: 'The woman I lived with was not permitted to stay at my side. They took her away because she was a hindrance to my marriage. My heart, which was deeply attached to her, was pierced, and wounded so that it bled. She returned to Africa and

2   i.e. God. *Confessiones* was written as Augustine's
     confessions to God.

3   Conf. VI, 15.

4   Floria uses the Latin name *Mediolanum*.

5   Augustine's mother.

promised you[2] she would never live with another man. She left with me our natural son.'[3]

It is good to see you can still remember how closely we two were once bound together. You know our union was something more than the kind of fleeting cohabitation customary before the man marries. We lived faithfully together for more than twelve years and had a son together. Quite often it happened that people we met took us to be man and wife according to the law. And you liked that, Aurel, I think it made you a little proud, for many men are ashamed of their wives. Can you remember when we walked together across the River Arno? Just suddenly you stopped me with a hand on my shoulder. Then you said something to me. Can you remember it?

Several times you write that there are many things you leave out and that you have forgotten a great deal. You must forgive me if I help you on one or two important points.

It is true that I made the promise not to know any other man. But I did not make that promise to God. Wasn't it you who begged me to make *you* that promise? I am sure about this, for it was my only consolation when I travelled home alone from Milan.[4] You still cared – a little anyway – about me. And perhaps Monica[5] would change her mind, perhaps we two would put our arms around each other again. For one doesn't ask for fidelity from someone one rejects in hatred or anger. A little further on you write: 'My wound, inflicted when my relationship with the woman I lived with was brought to

an end, would not heal either. At first it was inflamed and terribly painful, but then it festered, and I grew less sensitive to pain.'[6] Ah, well, I shall return to that sensitivity and pain, and to the festering.

As we both know, I wasn't torn away from you just because Monica had found a suitable girl. Naturally that was Monica's reasoning, she was thinking of the future of the family. Or was she a little jealous of me too? That was something I often pondered on. I can't forget that spring when she came sweeping into Milan and somehow put herself between us.

But it was the two of you who sent me away, and for you it was not chiefly on account of the planned marriage, it was for another reason as well. You thrust me from you because you loved me too much, you said. It's normal, of course, to stand by a loving partner, but you did the opposite thing. It was because you had already started to disdain passionate love between man and woman. You thought I bound you to the world of the senses so you had no peace and quiet in which to concentrate on the salvation of your soul. In consequence nothing came of this proposed marriage either. God desires above all that man should live in abstinence, you write. I have no faith in such a God.

What unfaithfulness, Aurel! What a sublime betrayal you were guilty of when you sent me away! In your heart you cleaved to me, and your heart was wounded so that it bled. My heart suffered the same hurt, naturally, if that signifies anything, for we were two souls who were torn from each other, or two bodies if you wish, or in

7   *O tempora, O mores!* Cicero makes use of the
    expression several times in his orations. Floria's
    constant allusions to Roman writers and
    philosophers may indicate that she wishes to
    emphasise that she is now a well-read woman.

fact two souls in one body. Your wound would not heal, it was inflamed and terribly painful until eventually it festered and you grew less sensitive to pain. But why? Well, because you loved the salvation of your own soul more than you loved me. What times, esteemed Bishop, what manners![7]

Have you never thought through what happened in this way? From your confessions it does not seem so. But isn't it precisely an intensified form of infidelity to desert one's beloved for the sake of saving one's own soul? Wouldn't it be easier for a woman to bear if the man left her because he wanted to marry – or because he preferred another woman, for that matter? But there was no other woman in your life, you merely loved your own soul more than me. Your own soul, Aurel, that was what you wanted to save, that which once had found rest in me. You never had any particular desire to get married, not as long as you had me, you said, this marriage was merely a filial duty. And you never did marry. Your bride was not of this world.

Then there was our son, and as God is my witness: I was as much mother of Adeodatus as you were his blood father. It was I who bore him, and it was I who fed him at my breast, for we had no wet nurse. Then I left him with you, you write. No mother does this willingly, she does not desert her only son without suffering the most agonising grief. But without you beside me I could make no demands, for I had no fortune. Wasn't that why Monica wanted to have you married to a girl of high

8   I have been unable to discover which Greek writer
    Floria refers to.

standing? I think it was a Greek who said that 'justice is done only among equals'.[8]

In Book Nine you beseech God to accept your confessions including the innumerable things you pass over in silence. One of these omissions is our last meeting, and perhaps it is precisely that which you have in mind, for you do not say a word about what you did in Rome for a whole year before you came back to Africa. When you make such a great effort to write down your confessions, I think this omission is almost disgraceful.

What do you think now about what happened in Rome? How could it happen to us, Aurel? Perhaps it was actually in that wretched room up on the Aventine that your spiritual soul-searching was to begin. I am sure you heard I had managed to get to Ostia more or less safe and sound. There I obtained passage almost at once, and the voyage itself, considering the circumstances, went well, at least I arrived back in Carthage. This time too it was you who took care of the transportation. It was the second time I was sent back to Africa, almost like a piece of merchandise. It is long ago now, and the wounds have healed.

Ever since I came back from Milan almost fifteen years ago, I have walked in your footsteps. Or perhaps I should say I have retraced our old paths in Carthage. First I read everything I could get hold of on philosophy. For I had to find out what there was in philosophy that could divide a loving pair from each other. If you had become attached to another woman I might have wanted to see her. But my rival was not another woman I could see

9   *Obitus veneris*, i.e. the annihilation of love.

10   Conf. VIII, 11.

11   *Multa paucis*.

12   *Dum vitant stulti vitia in contraria currunt.*

13   Cicero (106–43 BC), Roman statesman, orator and
     philosopher, contributed a great deal in spreading
     the knowledge of Greek philosophy in Rome. As a
     philosopher he can best be characterised as an
     eclectic, i.e. one who seeks to fuse the best of
     various philosophical systems into one. The text to
     which Augustine refers in *Confessiones, Hortensius*, is
     now lost.

14   Conf. III, 4.

15   Floria plays on an expression taken from the satires
     of Juvenal (*Vitam impendere vero*).

with the naked eye, she was a philosophical principle. So in order to understand you better I had to go some way along the same road you had trodden. I had to read philosophy.

My rival was not only *my* rival. She was every woman's rival, she was love's own angel of death.[9] You yourself refer to her as Abstinence. Book Eight, Aurel! You write: 'Then I was given to see abstinence in her pure beauty, serene and cheerful, but without frivolity in her joy. With appealing friendliness she bade me come without hesitation. Then she stretched out her pious hands to receive and embrace me.'[10]

Here you write a great deal in very few words![11] You do not even try to conceal how you allowed yourself to be seduced. I cannot deny that my heart boiled with jealousy when I read that particular section. For wasn't it in somewhat the same fashion that you gave yourself to me when we were aglow with youth? Wasn't it with 'appealing friendliness' that I tried to embrace you? I feel like saying with Horace: When foolish people want to avoid making a mistake they do the opposite thing![12]

I began with Cicero[13] as you did. In your Book Three you write about him: 'But there was one thing in particular I loved in Cicero's exhortation: it did not spur me on to seek this or that philosophical direction, but to love and seek and win truth itself . . .'[14] And truth, Aurel, it is that which has spurred me to read the philosophers and the great poets. I have read the four gospels as well. Since we were torn apart, I have devoted my life totally to Truth[15] – as you once set out to devote yourself to

16 A play on the following statement, according to
    tradition derived from Aristoteles: *Amicus Plato, sed
    magis amica veritas* (Plato is dear to me, but truth is
    still more dear).

17 I would think that here Floria is thinking of
    philosophical writings by other authors.

18 *Feminis lugere honestum est, viris meminisse.*

Abstinence. You are still dear to me, although I must add that today truth is still more dear.[16] Now I pass as a learned woman who gives private lessons here in Carthage. Don't you think that's quite amusing to think of, by the way – that now it is I who am the teacher of rhetoric? Or have you lost your sense of humour too? There isn't much humour in your confessions, Aurel. It wasn't like that with the two of us. We could laugh and joke from sunset to sunrise. Today you'd probably say humour is the same as 'sensual passion' or 'self-indulgence'.

All the same, I must thank you for your books. No other writings[17] have helped me to understand better why you first wanted to part from me because you intended to wait until an eleven-year-old girl became old enough to marry you – and then later chose to worship the goddess you call Abstinence. I am grateful that you write so frankly and sincerely. That your memory can play tricks with you now and then is quite another matter, and that is one of the reasons for my writing. Tacitus wrote that it is fitting for women to grieve over a loss, for men to remember it.[18] But you don't even remember, Aurel!

I have three letters in front of me. You sent one of them from Milan as soon as you had decided not to get married after all. It was not so many months after I had had to leave. Then I received your letter from Ostia when Monica died. How sweet of you to allow Adeodatus to add a little message to his mother. A year or two later I had another letter. It was after the poor lad

19 Conf. IX, 6.

20 He who is given by God.

was taken from you. Did anyone see you weep at that time? For I assume you don't believe the boy fell sick and died because he was conceived in sin? The reason I ask this is because of something you write in your Book Nine. Here you refer to Adeodatus as 'the fruit of my sin'. True, you add that God 'has power to make something beautiful out of our abomination'.[19] For you had no other part in the boy than sin, you write. You should be ashamed of yourself, Aurel, you who gave him the name of Adeodatus![20] Surely you don't believe the Lord did away with the boy to help you in your career as priest and bishop? May he look mercifully upon your delusions!

A son dies, Aurel. I think you should have come to me so we could have wept a little together, you and I. You were not yet ordained, nor were you betrothed, and Adeodatus was our only son. But perhaps you were so full of shame for what had happened in Rome that you didn't have the courage to meet me? Or were you afraid the same thing might happen again?

I can't understand at all why you find it so difficult to weep. Book Nine, Aurel! Do you really think it is too carnal a thing to show grief? You would not even allow your own son to let his tears flow freely when he had to bid farewell to his grandmother! I feel it must be more 'carnal' to hold back the tears, for when we do not have a good cry the grief will often stay inside us like a heavy burden. Peace be with the boy's memory!

II

21   Although Seneca does say one should listen to the other side, in Floria's letter this is differently phrased. Here this dialectical principle is formulated exactly as it was transmitted through Augustine's words *audiatur et altera pars* in his text *De duabus animabus* from 391. Floria may have known this work. I myself prefer to meditate on the possibility that it is Augustine who in *De duabus animabus* expresses himself in Floria's words at the Forum Romanum in the winter of 388.

22   Conf, I, 2. Cf. Rom. 11, 36.

As I mentioned, I was able to borrow your confessions from the priest here in Carthage. Forgive me now for copying out some sections that I shall comment on further. I hope you have the patience to read my reflections with an open mind. Or my confessions if you like. For I regard this letter as something more than a personal greeting from me to you, it is also a letter to the Bishop of Hippo Regius. Years have passed, and much has changed since we two had our arms around each other. Thus what I write will perhaps be equally a letter to the whole Christian church, for today you are a man of great influence.

I must admit that this very thought alarms me, but I pray to God that a woman's voice too may be heard by men of the church. You may perhaps recall something I said to you that morning we walked down at the Forum Romanum and saw the thin layer of snow covering the Palatine. I talked of Seneca's tragedy *Medea* which I had just read. In the play it says that the other side too should be heard, and that was me.[21]

The first book begins so promisingly as you praise God for his wisdom and grandeur. 'For of you, and through you, and in you are all things,' you write.[22] Then you talk about your early childhood, although I think you borrow

29

23 Conf. I, 7.

24 Conf. I, 11.

many of your observations from Adeodatus's first years. But already here we find the sombre undertones that run like a red thread through all your books: 'To you, no one is pure and free from sin, not even the infant who lives but one day on earth ... the helpless infant limbs may be innocent, but not the infant soul.' And why not? Well, because you have seen a little boy who 'white with fury and with a spiteful expression' looked over at his brother who also wanted the breast. Poor Aurel! Because the child wants the breast, it does not indicate he is wicked! And you write too that God has 'endowed the body with senses and limbs, adorned it with a beautiful form and implanted in it all the instincts that will sustain and defend life.'[23] But you do not dwell on this as something beautiful and good, straightaway you start fretting again about being born in iniquity and your mother conceiving you in sin. Or in love, honoured Bishop, the child is conceived in love, God ordained the world so beautifully and wisely, he did not allow it to happen by germination.

You even think you can see a deeper meaning in the fact that Monica did not have you baptised as a child. 'For those spots of sin one contracted after the bath of baptism would certainly bring with them greater and more dangerous guilt.'[24] Sin and guilt – because God created us man and woman with a rich register of senses and needs. Or with instincts, if you will, or with titillating desires, Aurel, I can say it as it is to you, you who once were my little itchy-fingered bedfellow. Even your youthful predilection for the story of Dido and Aeneas you add to your lifelong list of sins.

25   Manicheeism was a religious movement which had
     great influence in Augustine's time. It had a half
     religious, half philosophical doctrine of salvation
     based on the dualist idea that the world is divided
     between good and evil, light and dark, spirit and
     matter. Man could rise above the material world
     with the aid of the spirit and thus lay the
     foundation for the soul's salvation.

26   Conf. X, 32.

27   *Plaudite!* i.e. 'Congratulations!'

28   Conf. X, 31.

29   *Dulce est desipere in loco.*

You constantly write like this about 'sensual lust' and 'sinful desires' throughout all your books. Has it occurred to you that it might be you who look on God's gifts with scorn? It strikes me that your contempt for the world of the senses may derive from the Manichees[25] and the Platonists rather than from the Nazarene himself.

In your Book Ten you are unreserved in emphasising your contempt not only for the world of the senses, and thus for God's work of creation, but for the senses themselves – which also are God's work of creation, I would think: 'The temptations of the sense of smell do not greatly appeal to me. When they are absent, I do not seek them; if they are present, I do not disdain them, but am prepared to go without them for ever.'[26] You are even ashamed because sometimes you catch yourself eating food because you find it good. But now God has taught you 'to use foodstuffs in the same way as one takes medicine'. I congratulate you[27] – although the mere thought is nauseating to me. 'Even when we eat for the sake of our health, a dangerous feeling of wellbeing is at our heels,' you write. So it is 'not always easy to know whether it is the necessary consideration for the sustenance of the body, or the deceptive desire for pleasure that demands service'.[28] No, alas, Bishop, for what if something is both good for the gullet and healthy for the body at one and the same time! I myself turn to these simple words of Horace, and I do it with the easiest conscience in the world: 'It is comforting to let oneself go now and again.'[29]

You have to eat, Aurel, and you are permitted to

30   *Nihil tam absurdum dici potest ut non dicatur a*
     philosopho.

31   Conf. II, 1.

32   Conf. II, 2.

enjoy your food. You have not given up washing as well? When you see a lovely flower you may feel free to go and smell it. Even if today you call that 'the desire of the body'. You should be ashamed of yourself. But 'nothing is so absurd that it cannot have been said by a philosopher', writes Cicero.[30] The same thing could quite certainly be said of the theologians. Do you remember when we walked together across the River Arno? On the bridge you suddenly stopped because you wanted to smell my hair. Why did you want to do that, Aurel? Was it 'the desire of the body' making itself felt again? I do not believe that, no, I believe you once knew what real love is, but I am afraid you may have forgotten it.

In Book Two you write about your youthful years in Tagaste when your 'soul was corrupted by sensual lust'.[31] You write: 'The chief thing that gave me pleasure was loving and being loved ... But from the mud of physical attraction and from the source of youthful urges foggy vapours rose and left my heart in darkness and fog so that I could not distinguish between pure love and impure lust. Both feelings raced within me in blended confusion and dragged me, unsteady youth, down into an abyss of passions and pulled me under into a maelstrom of vices.'[32]

I think you brag a little, Aurel. Like most young lads you certainly had a lively imagination, but when I met you some years later it was a rather fumbling and inexperienced fellow I shared a bed with. You write too that you were ashamed not to have as much experience as your companions maintained they had. They boasted of their 'shameful vices', you write, so you did the same

35

33 Play on the well-known quotation from Terence:
Homo sum; nihil humanum a me alienum puto (I am a
human being and consider that nothing human is
alien to me).

34 Conf. II, 6.

35 Conf. II, 2.

36 Floria's indignation over Augustine extracting this
one verse from its context seems understandable.
See 1, Corinthians 7, 1–7.

thing yourself. Yes, that sort of thing is childish, don't you agree? But shameful? Perhaps the most shameful thing of all is that the Bishop of Hippo Regius is still preoccupied with such childish pranks. A bishop should not find any human manifestation strange,[33] and boys will be boys, they always have been. You aren't even averse to mentioning that frightful 'crime' you committed in your sixteenth year when, with a couple of other boys, you stole some pears from a pear tree.[34]

Then you suddenly grow more serious. First you refer to Paul's words about it being 'good for a man not to touch a woman'.[35] And, dear Aurel, why do you cite only this one verse? I think it is owing to something you have brought with you from the Manichees. Did you not learn at the school of rhetoric how dangerous it can be to detach a single sentence from its context? It is true that Paul writes that it can be good for a man not to touch a woman, but, he goes on, in order to avoid fornication every man should have his own wife and every woman her own husband. He emphasises further that woman and man shall be one body and constantly give themselves to each other so that neither shall be tempted into unfaithfulness because they cannot manage to live in abstinence.[36]

The question is whether it is especially wise to believe that one can be redeemed from 'sinful vices' by choosing Abstinence. Rather the opposite if you ask me. Truth to tell, you seem more absorbed in that kind of thing than most men of your age, although it is almost fifteen years since you threw yourself into the arms of Mother

37 *Naturam expellas furca, tamen usque recurret.*

38 Conf. II, 2. Cf. Matthew 19, 12. This verse in
    Matthew inspired a few early Christians to castrate
    themselves, among them the church father Origenes
    (185–254). In the *Vulgate*, the Latin translation of
    the Bible used by Augustine, the verse is translated
    thus: *Sunt enim eunuchi qui de matris utero sic nati
    sunt; et sunt eunuchi qui facti sunt ab hominibus; et sunt
    eunuchi qui se ipsos castraverunt propter regnum caelorum;
    qui potest capere capiat.*

39 Conf. X, 30.

40 From Sophocles's tragedy *King Oedipus*. When
    Oedipus finally realised he had killed his father
    (Laius) and married his mother (Jocasta), he gouged
    out both his eyes with Jocasta's ornamental pin.

Abstinence. Oh well, you did suffer a rather sizeable relapse, of course. If you drive nature out with a hayfork it will still return again, writes Horace.[37] Unless you deal with it more severely, for here it comes: you write that it would have been best if in your youth you had castrated yourself for the sake of the kingdom of heaven.[38] For then you could have waited for the embrace of God with a happier mind. Poor Aurel! How ashamed you are of being a man, you who were my little stallion. Even now – and this is many years after you chose Abstinence as your bride – even now you pour out your heart to the Lord and say you still miss a woman at your side. In Book Ten, Bishop, you write: 'But in my memory, that I have talked so much about now, there still live images of these things that have lodged there from old habit. They force themselves upon me, not vividly, it is true, when I am awake; but in sleep they tempt me, not only to pleasure, but to assent and to act upon them.'[39]

I gather from these confessions that you have not yet castrated yourself. Can it even be that now and again you miss me? Can it be the memories of me and our old 'habits' that come to you in your dreams? For you have certainly not done *that*, Aurel? You who were once my proud bedpost. Why couldn't you just as well have blinded yourself? Oedipus did.[40] Why couldn't you cut off your tongue? For I am sure you still long for my kisses.

I think when all is said and done that your sex too was a sense organ. Wasn't it, Aurel? Anyway, you are the one who keeps on writing about 'sensual lust' when what you

have in mind is the delights of love. Or do you believe that your eyes and ears are more divinely created than your sex? Do you think some parts of the human body are less worthy of God than others? For instance, is your middle finger more neutral than your tongue? You did use your finger too!

III

III

IN BOOK THREE you write of the time you came to Carthage as a young student: 'A vicious erotic life boiled around me on all sides, exactly like a witches' cauldron. I was not yet in love, but I longed for love. I kept my desires hidden and felt irritated with myself because I had so little craving. Out of the need for love I searched for something I could love.'[41]

Then you found me. You had only been in the town a year when we met, I myself was born here. We were both in our nineteenth year. I remember I was sitting beneath a fig tree with three or four students. You already knew one of them and came walking towards us, so I squinted against the sun and looked up at you. I must have done that in a manner that captivated you, for you held my gaze, but glanced down at the ground irresolutely once or twice before you searched for my eyes again. It almost felt as if we two had lived a life together already. I knew at once that I could come to love you with heart and soul. Yet I could neither have feared nor dreamed that it would happen that same night, although if I had surmised it I might perhaps have done both at the same time.

It was not so strange that I was with some students, but you noticed with some astonishment that I took part in

45

42 From Vergil's *Aeneid*. Aeneas makes land at
    Carthage after a shipwreck and engages in a
    passionate love affair with Dido, Queen of
    Carthage. But Aeneas has a great project awaiting
    him. He frees himself from Dido's embraces and
    sets course for Italy to establish an extensive
    kingdom, the later Rome. He does this without
    showing any pity for Dido and her tragic fate. Her
    broken heart leads her to take her own life in the
    sorrows of love.

the conversation just like one of them. And that was one of the first things we talked about as soon as you and I were alone together. At first we discussed Vergil with the students, then life and love in general. I seem to recall that you noted with some surprise how naturally I defended Dido's deed of love.[42] It was as if you asked me with your eyes whether a woman could really love a man so deeply that she could come to take her own life if she was betrayed.

I don't know whether it was because we talked of Dido and Aeneas that you then suddenly asked me if I had been to Rome. Anyway, I thought it was a strange question, very strange, for we two had never known each other, and yet you wanted to know if I had been in Rome. I think I interpreted it as a way of courting, for you were quick to say you had not yet been there yourself, but that you planned to go one day. Since we had just been talking of Dido, it was as if by this question you made me into the Queen of Carthage herself sitting there, and since I had defended this legendary queen so fervently it was almost as if you wanted to say that if only I were yours you would want me to go to Rome with you, you would never let me suffer the same fate as hers. At that time I did not know that many years later the two of us really would journey to Rome together. But it seemed somehow that Aeneas's leaving Carthage was where it all began. Perhaps I should add that it was here everything ended as well. Like Aeneas, you too had a mission which was greater and more important than love in Carthage.

47

In the end we were left sitting by ourselves beneath the fig tree. Already then and there I think there must have been something about the two of us that somehow frightened the others, something strong and close, as if we were invisible conspirators. Then you went back with me to my little room, and stayed the night there. Eighteen months later we had a son, and we were inseparable until Monica or Abstinence tore us away from each other and left us both with bleeding wounds.

From the beginning our life together was firmly grounded on sensuality, for we certainly cultivated Venus together, at times we were both equally unstoppable. When I read your confessions today, though, I have a sad feeling that what you now call the sensual was the only thing that bound the two of us to each other. It may seem as if you are almost over-zealous where repentance and remorse for your earlier life are concerned, and thus for the time before you dedicated yourself wholly to Abstinence. Is it really God or is it just as much your own doubt and remorse you are trying to exorcise?

Perhaps it is precisely our deep friendship you are most ashamed of. There are many men who feel more ashamed of cultivating a woman's friendship than of devoting themselves to a sensual love relationship with her. Then they are likely to blame the sensual love for their being unable to cultivate any sincere friendship with a woman as well. Unfortunately, the more philosophically schooled they are, the more tangible this is; I attribute much of the blame to the Manichees and the Platonists. I think you looked at me in a new way after

49

43 The *Phaedo*, dialogue by Plato in which Socrates
    discusses the arguments for the immortality of the
    soul.

44 Porphyrius (232–304), neo-platonic philosopher,
    pupil of Plotinus.

45 After Horace: *Quot capita, tot sensus.*

46 Ambrosius (339–397) held a high position in the
    service of the state before being appointed Bishop
    of Milan.

47 Conf. III, 1.

you had read the *Phaedo*,[43] and it was no better after you
had read Porphyrius.[44] So many heads, Aurel, so many
opinions![45] But I did not suspect real trouble until you
started calling me Eve, but that was not until we had
gone to Milan. It was when you did whatever you could
to get entry into the circle around Ambrosius.[46]

You yourself write that your soul was not strong and
well at that time. 'Covered with abscesses it threw itself
out into misery, desiring to ease its itch with sensual
pleasures. But even these were not entirely without soul;
otherwise I would never have loved them. I felt it was
delightful both to love and be loved, especially when I
was able to possess the beloved bodily. Thus I soiled the
deep springs of friendship with impure sensual lust, and
dulled its clear radiance with a hellish allure.'[47]

So you do not hide how deeply and fervently you now
despise Venus. She, Aurel, who herself was the jewelled
bridge between our two lonely and fearful souls. But that
is not all. Now you despise all other sensual joys too. And
more, more: you go on to despise the senses themselves.
Truly, you have become a eunuch!

I do not understand how you can sweep away our
secrets simply by calling them 'sensual lust' or 'the lust for
pleasure'. Well, I did not understand it before I read in
your Book Ten that today you despise all the senses and
everything they offer of fruit and wine to our souls. But
this is not all. You start to boast to God about how
deeply you can now realise that you despise the whole of
his work of creation. You do this because of a 'radiance'
you say you have seen with your inner eye.

Primum esse, tum philosophari.

In any case I shall not forget your playful hands and your witty repartee. I see you have lost your way among the theologians. What a miserable occupation! How can the small preside over the great? How can the work define the master? Indeed, how can the work determine that it shall stop functioning as a work?

We are created human beings, Aurel. And we are created man and woman. In his writings on age Cicero says something about the youth not wishing for the strength of the lion or the elephant. We should not try to live as something other than what we are. Would that not be to mock God? We are human beings, Aurel. We must first live, and then – yes, then we can philosophise.[48]

Was I nothing more than a woman's body to you? You know that isn't true. And how can you distinguish between body and soul? Isn't that bungling God's work of creation? Oh yes, it certainly is, my own faithless tiger. When you clawed me with your sharp caresses, you were also tearing at my soul.

You describe friendship so beautifully in your Book Four, but then, of course, it is only friendship with men you have in mind: 'We talked and laughed together and were mutually obliging. Sometimes we read well-written books; sometimes we joked with each other, sometimes we exchanged civilities. Occasionally we disagreed, but with no animosity, rather as when a man disagrees with himself. But that kind of rare difference of opinion merely served to spice the unanimity which generally prevailed. We taught each other and learned from each

49 Conf. IV, 8.

other. When some of us were absent we longed for them almost painfully, and welcomed them joyfully on their return. With these and similar signs the love of friends can pass from heart to heart, through facial expression, words and glances and a thousand friendly gestures. They were like sparks that set our souls on fire and fused the many into one.'[49]

When I read that section I felt almost as if I'd been eaten up – or in some way both eaten up and regurgitated at one and the same time. For weren't these words equally applicable to our friendship? We talked and laughed together and were mutually obliging – from sunset to sunrise. It was we who sent each other little secret signals 'from heart to heart, through facial expression, words and glances and a thousand friendly gestures'. Now it is as if you take the best things from our life together and somehow dare to preserve them in memory by isolating them to friendship between men. You were not quite so larcenous at the time we met each other beneath the fig tree. Certainly you did have a lot of friends then, exceptionally many, even. But the love we two entertained for each other was of another kind, so I was never jealous of your men friends. Sparks were struck between us which not only set our souls on fire but also ignited our bodies.

You don't exactly neglect to confess your remorse for our sensual love, and be that as it may, although you must not on that account forget that I was your best friend as well. For you sank so deep into the mud that you cultivated friendship with a woman. For I was not merely

50 *Scortum*, skin; the word can also mean 'prostitute, whore'.

51 *Delictum*.

52 *Peccatum*.

53 Here Floria paraphrases an old Roman marriage formula.

flesh and blood.[50] Your greatest offence[51] then was not that you loved a woman in the flesh, in that respect you were neither better nor worse than most. Your most outrageous sin[52] was that you loved Eve's soul as well.

If it were not because you yourself entreated God so earnestly to examine your heart, I should not bother to remind you of these bygone things, for it is a long time since we two had our arms around each other. But it seems as if you let Truth ride like an untamed foal through your confessions. And let it run, Aurel, let it run all the way home to me. It will find rest there, for I am the only one who knows it.

Perhaps there may be a God who knows us. If so, I am quite sure he has stored up all the goodness we two gave each other. And if he doesn't exist, my old twin soul, then there can be none in the whole universe who know each other better than you and I. For you gave me body and soul, just as I pledged myself body and soul to you. Where you were, I was, and where I was, there you wanted to be.[53] Then first a mother came between us, then came the Manichees and the Platonists, and finally you put the theologians and Abstinence between us. Thus in a way you travelled even further away from me than Aeneas had travelled from Dido. May God look mercifully on your errors.

Were you and I not two sides of a body that fused together – as a bridge joins the two sides of a river into one body? Then a mighty divinity suddenly rises up from the river – or an abstract principle of Abstinence – that seems to sever the connection between one river bank

and the other? No, I do not believe in such a God, your Grace. This is something I have discussed with the priest of Carthage many times. He knows that I once lived with a man, but not that it was you. So didn't it seem like something torn out of a tragedy when suddenly one morning he came to me with your confessions? Or was it something you had suggested to him?

Can you still remember how you stroked me all over and seemed to tighten every bud before it opened itself? How you enjoyed plucking me! How you allowed yourself to be intoxicated by my perfumes! How you nourished yourself on my juices! And then you went away and sold me for the sake of your soul's salvation. What infidelity, Aurel, what guilt! No, I don't believe in a God who demands human sacrifices. I don't believe in a God who lays waste a woman's life to save a man's soul.

IV

54 Conf. III, 12.

55 i.e. Augustine.

56 Conf. III, 11.

WE SOON MOVED, with our little boy, he was just two, to Tagaste, your birthplace, where you began to teach rhetoric. Towards the end of Book Three you write: 'Incidentally, I leave out a great deal here, because I am hastening to get to the things which are most pressing for me to confess to you. I have also forgotten much.'[54]

But surely you haven't forgotten how hard it was for Monica to have you living in her house with Adeodatus and me? Already then I felt that you and Monica were bound together by ties that are unnatural between mother and son. I had my own ideas about Monica's visions, you know. She dreamed 'she was standing on a treetrunk. A young man came up to her, radiant with happiness, and he smiled at her as she stood there burdened with sorrow. He asked why she grieved and wept every day. He did this, as is usual with such visions, to manifest something to her, not to question her. She replied that she was lamenting because I was lost. Then he begged her not to worry, and urged her to pay heed and she would come to see that where she was, there was I also.[55] And when she looked up she could see that I stood beside her on the same treetrunk.'[56]

You repeat this, Aurel – as if to make what you have

57 Cf. footnote 53. Augustine's expression 'where you
    were, there I was' for many people in Augustine's
    time must have held associations with the
    relationship of man and woman in marrige.

58 Conf. IX, 12.

59 Cf. footnote 40. Unaware of what he is doing,
    Oedipus marries his own mother (Jocasta) with
    whom he has four children.

60 *Furor poeticus*, i.e. 'poetic frenzy'.

61 *Ridendo dicere verum*, from Horace's satires.

on your mind even clearer: 'Where you are, there he is also.'[57] You and Monica then, mother and son on the same treetrunk. Perhaps it was chiefly religion that was alluded to here, although it looks now as if you are reading more into it. Should not a man leave his father and mother, live with a woman, and the two become one flesh? She placed herself between us, and it was she who finally won the duel, she certainly was a powerful woman, with great ambition for herself and her son.

But let us hasten on to Book Nine. You write of your own grief when Monica died at Ostia: 'It was as if my life was torn to shreds. For her life and mine had become one.'[58]

But, Aurel! Have you no shame? Have you quite forgotten Oedipus and Jocasta?[59] Oh, well, he blinded himself, and you wish you had castrated yourself, perhaps it comes to the same thing. Poet's frenzy,[60] Aurel! Now and again it's rather tempting to tell the truth with a joke.[61]

Nevertheless you felt a void in your life at that time, and – as it seemed to me – you sent for me. It didn't take you long to put God in your mother's place. It seemed he was the only thing left to you after her departure, a new mother. For to begin with Monica was with you in place of God, and now you seem to have God with you in her place. To begin with it was she who came between you and me, later it was the God of the Nazarene who held that place.

I have asked myself many times whether in reality it was your own mother who stole from you the will to

62   *Vita brevis.*

63   The quotation continues thus in Conf. IV, 2: 'In
      cohabiting with her I was certainly able to learn by
      my own experience the difference there is between
      a marriage grounded on the idea of having children,
      and a love relationship engaged in purely to satisfy
      one's own passion, so that the children born of it
      are not wished for, even though one is obliged to
      love them once they have arrived.' Clearly, Floria
      was so unimpressed by this passage that she does
      not even trouble to comment on it. Her emphasis
      is on the contrary experience, namely that they
      lived together as spouses.

love a woman. Wasn't it because you loved me that from the start Monica was reluctant to live in the same house as you and eat at the same table? Book Three, Aurel. Wasn't it also because of that that she went running to Milan wanting to get you married? Book Six! And wasn't it for that same reason that you chose Abstinence when nothing came of the planned marriage after all?

After we had walked across the River Arno you stopped me with an affectionate hand on my shoulder and asked if you could smell my hair. 'Life is so short,'[62] you said. Why did you say that, Aurel? And why did you want to smell my hair? What was it you wanted to seal?

It is not until the beginning of Book Four that you mention me. You write: 'In those years I had a woman and lived with her, but not in what is called lawful marriage. She fell prey to my unstable and ill-considered passion. But I did have only the one, and I was faithful to her as to a spouse.'[63]

When I read this section on your unstable and ill-considered passion, I had to laugh aloud, for I felt your passion was both stable and considered, I really did. Moreover it was constant, although at times it could burn less brightly than at others. Besides, I was certainly no 'prey'. As you yourself intimate, we lived like a married couple – with the one vital difference that we had declared ourselves to each other without interference from parents. If you hadn't loved me you would undoubtedly have taken other women, or gone to a brothel for that matter. We were not married, everyone would have understood if you had chosen another

64 Augustine does not give the friend's name.

65 Conf. IV, 6.

66 Conf. IV, 7.

concubine in my place. But the only thing that stood between us was Monica – and gradually your nagging conscience telling you that perhaps you cultivated our love so fervently that it might stand in the way of your soul's salvation.

Now you write about Claudius[64] who died of fever. 'I was miserable, and miserable is every soul bound by love to that which perishes ... I was dreadfully weary of life and at the same time fearful of death.'[65] Then you write: 'I carried a shattered and bleeding soul which found it unbearable to be in me; but I could find nowhere to give it rest. It did not find peace in pleasant groves, nor in games and song, nor in scented flower gardens, nor in glittering feasts, nor in the enjoyment of sensual love, not even in books and poetry.'[66]

I well remember that time, for it was not easy for any of us. And yet: we had each other the whole time, and now that your friend was dead I was your only consolation. I believe it was then that you began to search in earnest for a truth that could save your soul from that which perishes. I said: Hold me close. Life is so short, and we cannot be sure that there is any eternity for our frail souls. Perhaps this is our only life. You would never believe such a thing, Aurel. You would rack your brains until you found an eternity for your soul. It seemed more important to you to save it from perdition than it was to save mine.

So we left Tagaste and returned to Carthage. I rejoiced, for sharing a house with Monica was no life for us. You write: 'Days came, and days passed, and each day

that passed gave me fresh hope and new ideas, and so little by little I became myself again with the aid of the same joys as before.'[67] But the seed was sown, a new earnestness had taken possession of you.

It is strange that you do not write more about Adeodatus. Although perhaps you include him when you mention 'the same joys as before'?

V

IN BOOK FIVE you write about the journey from Carthage to Rome. 'My mother was terribly upset about my leaving and followed me out to the sea. She strove forcibly to hold me back, trying either to get me to go home with her or to take her with me.'[68] But we tricked her, Aurel. You took her to that chapel of Cyprian where she spent the night. Then we set sail in the dead of night, you and I and little Adeodatus, he was now a boy of eleven. I remember you joked and said that the Queen of Carthage was going to Rome with Aeneas. And when we sailed away from Carthage I really felt like a resurrected Dido. I thought of that strange question you had put to me more than ten years previously: Have you been to Rome? I was so sure that what we were doing was right. If the two of us were to have a future we would somehow have to free ourselves from Monica together.

Then you fell into a fever, but I nursed you and prayed for you. I remember how frightened you were of dying. Again and again you asked: 'Is it all up with me now? Am I lost?' For you had not yet found any salvation for your soul. You write: 'The fever rose, and I was about to die and be lost. Indeed, where would I have gone if I had passed away then? Yes, to the fire and the torments that

69   Conf. V, 9.

70   The perdition of the soul must not be confused
     with the Christian concept of the judgement of
     God. It was a widespread view within various
     philosophical movements throughout the whole of
     antiquity that some souls were damned while others
     could make themselves deserving of eternal life.

71   Stoicism was a philosophical movement that stresses
     spiritual equilibrium in harmony with the
     controlling intelligence of the world. The Stoics
     emphasised that all natural processes − as for
     instance disease and death − follow the inviolable
     laws of nature. The human being must therefore
     learn to resign himself to his fate.

my deeds deserved according to your rightful ordinance.'[69]

But by Hades, Aurel! Whatever is this but distorted mythology? You who have so fiercely ridiculed the stories of the old gods, then you still go on believing in a God of Wrath who will punish and torment people for their deeds throughout all eternity? It was lucky you did not believe in him when you lay ill in a little room in Rome. You were just so terribly frightened of your soul going to perdition.[70] It was I who had to try to soothe your fear with some words of comfort from the philosophy of the Stoics.[71] We also spoke of the Nazarene and the Christian hope. But neither of us came near to believing in this teaching of the fire and eternal torment. We were too sophisticated for that. But is that what an esteemed imperial rhetor does today? He thinks that in a few years the Bishop of Hippo Regius will be safe and sound in God's blissful paradise, while Floria Aemilia will be banished into eternal fire and torment because she hasn't yet consented to be baptised. No, your Grace, you will have to justify that teaching very quickly, if you don't I am not a little worried that still more people will be baptised and that the Universal Church will grow. We are both aware of the political decadence our community has undergone recently. Then it's probably not to be wondered at that customs and beliefs undergo a similar decadence!

You soon recovered. I haven't forgotten how suddenly the fever lost its grip, in only a moment you were on your feet again. Then we went out into town

72   i.e. the Sceptics. Augustine himself describes them
     in these words: 'They thought one should doubt
     everything, and declared that man cannot
     comprehend any truth.' (Conf. V, 10).

73   Florence.

together, you and I. For several months you taught rhetoric, at the same time finding nourishment in all the conversations with those philosophers who are called academics.[72] I was constantly allowed to accompany you, especially when you were going to meet new people. You were proud, proud as a victor to have me at your side, not so much because you had chosen me as because I had chosen you.

It was then you were appointed to the imperial post as tutor of eloquence in Milan. The journey there was a great experience, and that might well have been when we two had our richest hours together. Do you remember when we set out along the Via Cassia that fine autumn day – Adeodatus, you and I, and a couple of friends, Aurel, and all those we had not known before. We were a large company.

Then we arrived at the old garrison town of Florentia[73] on the River Arno. Can you remember how we stood there pointing up at the snow-covered mountains that were suddenly revealed through the trees? You only remember ideas, Aurel, can't you try to recall some real sense experiences too? Soon we walked across the river, and it was while we were still on the bridge that you came up behind me. You were engaged in conversation with some men, but then suddenly you were at my side. I felt your hand on my shoulder, then you pulled me gently towards you and whispered: 'Life is so short, Floria!'

Then you seized my wrist and held it tightly – as if you had decided that this moment was one you would never

forget. It was then you asked if you could smell my hair. You did so. I felt your breath on my neck while you untwisted my long hair and breathed in its scent. It was as if you wanted to draw the whole of me into yourself, as if I had my home within you. It felt as if you wanted to express something of how I would always belong with you because our souls had fused together. This was before Monica came to Milan, it was before those tiresome plans for marriage and before you met the theologians.

Now, do not come and say that what happened on the bridge over the Arno was merely the result of 'sensual passion' or 'self-indulgence', good Bishop. Many people were looking at us that day, and perhaps it is that very thing that makes me remember it so well. There on the bridge you suddenly did something you knew I set great store by, it was a gesture to me, an expression of your deep acknowledgement of me as the woman in your life, even though I was not your wife according to law. I also think it may have been an expression of release because at last we were able to move freely in a land far away from Monica. Were we not both in some way fugitives?

The years have gone by and much has happened since we two lived together in Italy, but the fact that you pleased me and yourself found pleasure in the scent of my hair now we were on our way out into the province together, would that cause your God to lay a curse on you? Was it to redeem such sins that he let his only son be nailed to the cross? We too had a son with us on that journey, he hopped and danced around his father and

74 Probably a paraphrase of the adage *Ubi mens plurima, ibi minima fortuna* (Where there is most intellect there is least money).

75 A precious stone, shell or other material carved in relief. A particularly popular art form in this period.

76 *Nil nisi bene.* Here she may play on the saying *De mortuis nil nisi bene* (Nothing but good of the dead). If this is so it must be interpreted as an insinuation that Aurel's soul is no longer a living soul.

77 *In Florentia Floria floruit.*

78 *Auro*, 'like gold'. Some of the wordplay is lost in translation.

mother – but nailed to a cross for the sake of love? I hope for your soul's salvation that your God has as well developed a sense of humour as you had before you met with the theologians. Even so he must have a more macabre sense of humour than yours, if not he may come to think that your soul has deteriorated so much since you walked over the River Arno with me that it is no longer possible to save. Where there is most intellect, your Grace, there as a rule is least love![74]

On the other side of the bridge we passed some vendors, and I stopped to look at a beautiful cameo.[75] Then you bought it for me, and now, now I sit with it in my hand. I clasp it, tightly. So God will have to forgive me for holding on to the 'physical'. But it is all I have. I haven't seen a radiant vision with my inner eye, nor have I seen anything supernatural or heard voices either, in that way I am still a simple woman. I wish you nothing but good for the salvation of your soul.[76] But life is short and I know so little. What if there is no heaven above us, Aurel, imagine that this life is what we were created for! Then, may our souls soar above the Arno for all eternity. For was it not in Florentia that Floria flourished,[77] and was it not in the evening sunshine over the Arno that Aurel's brow gleamed gold?[78]

VI

79 Conf. VI, 3.

80 Conf, V, 14.

81 Conf. VI, 11. Cf. footnote 72.

THEN, FINALLY, YOU met Bishop Ambrosius in Milan. You write that you thought him a fortunate man 'in the world's eyes because he was held in high esteem by powerful men'.[79] Only his unmarried state troubled you. Oh, such spiritual agony you had to go through because you allowed yourself more and more to be convinced that you would have to reject love itself for the sake of your soul's salvation!

Monica arrived in late spring, she had followed you over land and sea, you write. She placed herself facing you with her back to me, although she knew we were one. She had two aims, one was to have you baptised, the other to get you married to a girl of standing. I think the latter was the most important. You yourself were in doubt about everything, but you decided 'for the time being to become a catechumen in the Catholic Church, as my parents had advised me, until a light should appear by which I could confidently direct my course'.[80] In Book Six you exclaim: 'Oh, Academics, you who are such great men! Can we find no certainty to build our life on?'[81]

Now you must forgive me for copying out a rather long passage, but you show here that you did make a few sporadic attempts to collect your wits. You write: 'What

if death puts an end to all agony of soul at the moment it severs consciousness? Indeed, *that* is a question for discussion. But it cannot be like that. Far from it! It is not without reason that the Christian faith spreads and is so unusually highly regarded throughout the world. God would never have done such great and remarkable things for us if the death of the body was the end of the soul's life as well. Why do we still hesitate to relinquish all worldly hope and devote ourselves solely to seeking God and true happiness in life? But wait! After all, there are joys in this world as well, and they have their own charm, which is no small thing. We should not be too quick to put an end to our inclinations in that direction. For it would be somewhat unseemly to return to these pleasures later. Is it not a great achievement, to attain high position? What more then can one wish for? I have plenty of influential friends. If nothing else I could get a governorship – so as not to set my sights on something higher too quickly. Then I can take a wife with a substantial fortune, so she would not impose a heavier financial burden on me. That should be a suitable goal to aim for. Many great men worthy of taking as exemplars have devoted themselves to the study of wisdom even though they married. That was how I used to talk, and my heart was blown hither and thither by changing winds. Meanwhile time went by, and I delayed turning to the Lord. From day to day I postponed living in you, but I did not put off death from affecting me daily.'[82]

Life, that is, although here, true enough, you call life death, and it is you who do this, you who once bent over

83 Ibid.

84 *Nomina sunt odiosa*, i.e. 'names are objectionable',
    presumably taken from Cicero's speech to Roscius.

85 Friend and earlier pupil of Augustine, from
    Augustine's birthplace, Tagaste. Alypius went to
    Rome before Augustine did to study law. Then
    they journeyed together to Milan (Conf. VI, 7–10).

86 Conf. VI, 12.

87 Augustine must have gone through great agonies of
    soul when he deserted his partner, even though this
    is not touched upon in his *Confessiones*. There he
    does not give so much as a thought to the wounds
    he inflicted on Floria. But even in his text *De bono
    coniugali (On the Benefits of Marriage, 401)*, written
    at the time Augustine could have received the letter
    from Floria, he points out that a man who dismisses
    a faithful lover in order to marry another woman is
    guilty of infidelity. Not all Christians shared this
    view. It was generally accepted until well on into
    the Middle Ages that a man could have a
    concubine before he married. For example, Bishop
    Leo of Rome in the middle of the fifth century
    said it was permissible for a Christian man to leave
    a concubine in order to marry. This was not
    regarded as divorce or bigamy but on the contrary
    denoted moral improvement. Augustine, then,
    rejected such an idea. A man who has entered a
    relationship with a cohabitee should stay with his

me to smell my hair when we had walked over the River Arno together. You go on: 'I loved life's true happiness, but feared to seek it where it is to be found. And at the same time as I sought it, I fled from it. For I thought I would be far too unhappy if I had to go without a woman's embrace.'[83]

It was *my* embrace you could not do without, Aurel, that was something we two talked of many times. Couldn't you write it? Ah, well, one must be cautious about naming names.[84]

You also discussed such things constantly with Alypius:[85] 'Neither of us was especially attracted to what makes marriage into something beautiful, the task of creating a good home and bringing up children. The chief concern was that I was accustomed to satisfying my insatiable sexual desire, which kept me captive and plagued me violently.'[86]

What in reality plagued you was that a marriage – for which I was unfitted merely owing to my lack of worldly goods – would entail your betrayal of me. For were we not twin souls, Aurel, hadn't we grown so close both in body and soul that to divide us would be better left to a surgeon than to a mother playing the part of suitor? And didn't we also have Adeodatus to think of, he was twelve by then.[87]

You write: 'I was strongly advised to get married. I proposed and was accepted. My mother was enthusiastically absorbed in this. She wanted me first to get married and then be cleansed in the saving waters of baptism.'[88]

Then she sought me out. I can't forget the morning

partner and not go off and marry another woman later on.

I think it is interesting to question whether Augustine – so soon after writing *Confessiones* – would have adopted this view, which in fact defended the 'married' status or rights of the concubine, if he had not read the letter from Floria. So in the end perhaps she really was right in saying that her letter to Aurel was a letter to the whole Christian Church.

As recently as 1930 the Pope cited from Augustine's text *On the Benefits of Marriage*. Without realising it himself he may in a way have been influenced by Floria's letter. Although I may have my reasons for believing that both he and popes before him had been conversant with the *Codex Floriae*.

88 Conf. VI, 13.

89 *Peccatum*, fault or offence. Cf. Gr. *hamartia*, term for that error that eventually leads to the fall of the tragic hero. This kind of fatal fault is generally committed with the best of intentions, and it is precisely this which is the tragedy.

90 The Greeks used *himation*, not *toga*, the Latin name for Roman national costume. However, Floria uses the word *toga*.

91 *Sic, Aureli! Sic!*

Monica suddenly appeared in the room as I was washing. You had just left for the school of rhetoric and would be there all day. I was told to pack up and make myself scarce. Everything was arranged for the whole journey to Africa, a company was leaving that same afternoon. For you had proposed to a girl and been accepted. But the girl's parents had demanded that I should be removed from your side as fast as possible.

I thought that this was to be Monica's revenge for what had happened when we left her in Carthage that night. It seemed that now we were both to learn who was the strongest. But she said you had left it to her to get me out of the way because you couldn't bring yourself to do it. Like the peasant who can't bring himself to slaughter his own lamb. And I believed her, that was my tragic fault![89] For it must have struck you that I was that kind of tragic figure of a woman – as if drawn out of Euripides's toga.[90] I was betrayed by my own spouse for the sake of heavenly love! That is how it was, Aurel, that is exactly how it was![91]

I believed it was your premeditated wish that I was now to go back to Carthage, where once we had met each other beneath a fig tree. Not until we met again in Rome could you swear that I was sent away from you without your knowledge and will.

In her role as intermediary Monica also said you bade me promise not to live with any other man. I interpreted this as a sign that you had not yet really decided, and that perhaps we might come to hold each other again. To this day it has been a mystery to me why Monica should say

93

92 Must be a play on Cicero who ascribes the
    statement *Omnia mea mecum porto* to the Greek
    philosopher Bias, who was obliged to flee from his
    enemy without being able to take anything with
    him. But in fact he did take everything he
    possessed with him, i.e. it was only his wisdom and
    experience that was of any real value.

93 From Euripides's tragedy of Medea who killed her
    own children because her husband (Jason) deceived
    her. So Medea's hatred of Jason was stronger than
    her love for the children they had together. In their
    devastating passion Dido and Medea resemble each
    other not a little.

such a thing, for I was quite sure that all she had in mind was to get me away. Was it merely to make it slightly simpler for me to leave? Or perhaps she thought it would be easier for me to accept baptism if I didn't find another man to live with. But then I soon received the letter from you, in which you begged me so fervently not to give myself to anyone else. You even write that probably nothing will come of this marriage. But most important of all, you end the letter from Milan with these words: 'I miss you, Floria. Floria, I miss you!'

You had taken Adeodatus with you to the school of rhetoric that day, I wasn't even able to embrace him one last time before I had to pack up my possessions and part from man and child. So I took everything away with me.'[92]

I didn't do what Dido did, Aurel, so perhaps I promised too much that day beneath the fig tree. If I had had Adeodatus with me I would not have done what Medea did either.[93] But I went away.

VII

94 Conf. VI, 13. The usual marriageable age was
    12–13 years. We can thus assume – as Floria writes
    earlier – that she was only eleven.

YOU WRITE HOW eagerly Monica worked to have you married: 'The girl I had proposed to was about two years under marriageable age. But as I liked her, I was willing to wait.'[94] Well, I think you should have written that you liked waiting!

I myself find it rather disappointing that you don't append so much as a sentence or two on what you thought about your mother taking matters into her own hands and sending me away while you were out with Adeodatus. You went home to an empty house. And I – with whom you had travelled all the way from Africa – I had vanished. I, Aurel, with whom you had walked over the River Arno, I wasn't there any more. You merely write:

'The woman I lived with was not permitted to stay at my side. They took her away from me because she was a hindrance to my marriage. My heart, which was deeply attached to her, was pierced, and wounded so that it bled. She returned to Africa and promised you she would never live with any other man. She left with me our natural son. But I, unhappy man, could not follow her example. When I thought that there were still two years to wait before I could have the girl I had proposed to, I did not have the patience to wait. For though I did not

have a high opinion of marriage, I was a slave to my lust. Therefore I took another woman, but not as a wife. In this way my soul's sickness was unchanged, indeed, it grew even worse, as I waited for marriage, supported by old habit.'[95]

I had not heard a word about this other woman before I read your confessions. How ashamed you must have been, for I was not going to give myself to another. Still, it is useful to know about this, for here you are admitting that it was not precisely because you were to be married that I was sent away. Wouldn't it have been better for us to have had each other during the time you waited for the poor child to reach marriageable age? But you never wanted marriage, you wanted to save your soul from eternal annihilation, but then you had a perfectly ordinary relapse into 'sensual lust', and such things can happen. Poor you, Aurel, I begin to understand your profound need to make some sort of confession of sins, I am merely a little displeased with your selection.

I assume Monica did not frown on your new prey. She had managed to wipe out the years' long relationship with the woman you loved with heart and soul. So it was certainly a good substitute for the next woman merely to cover bodily 'sensual pleasure'. Your mother was a tolerant woman, your Grace, and nothing other than good must be said of the dead. In the end she took her cruel revenge for what had happened that night we two set sail from Africa.

You write: 'My wound, inflicted when my relationship with the woman I lived with was brought to an end,

96   Ibid.

97   Epicure (341–270 BC), Greek philosopher, resident
      of Athens. Epicure concurred with Democritus's
      atomism and believed materialistic philosophy could
      relieve the human fear of death and the punishment
      of the gods. 'Death does not concern us,' he said.
      'For as long as we live, death is not here. And
      when death comes, we are no longer alive.' He
      summed up his liberating philosophy with what he
      called the 'four healing herbs': 'The gods are not to
      be feared. Death is nothing to worry about. The
      good is easy to attain. The frightful is easy to bear.'

98   Conf. VI, 16.

99   I have been unable to discover which Greek Floria
      refers to.

100 Ariadne gave Theseus a ball of twine when he was
      about to enter the labyrinth on Crete (Knossos) to
      kill the monster Minotaur, which demanded seven
      girls and seven young men from Athens every
      ninth year. With the aid of the twine Theseus was
      able to find his way out of the labyrinth.

would not heal either. At first it was inflamed and terribly painful, but then it festered, and I grew less sensitive to pain. But the position grew more and more hopeless.'[96] And you go on: 'The only thing that kept me back from an even deeper maelstrom of sensual passions was the fear of death and your coming judgement, which never left my heart, however much I changed my views ... In my heart I would have given Epicure the prize[97] if I had not believed there was any life for the soul after death or any retribution for what we have done. But Epicure would not believe that. I asked: If we were immortal and could live in eternal sensual pleasure, without fear of losing it, why should we not be happy? And why should we seek for anything else?'[98]

No, why should we seek for anything else? I mean: Why should we search for something that may not exist? You remind me a little of that Greek who had won some gold coins in a game, then he wanted more and lost his whole fortune.[99]

Imagine a luxuriant landscape with people and animals, flowers and children, wine and honey. In this landscape there is also a frightful labyrinth. Now imagine, pious Bishop, you who were once my little playfully teasing bedfellow, imagine you have got lost inside this deep labyrinth. You can't find an Ariadne's thread[100] that can lead you out of the maze of paths and back to the paradise you were living in. But all the theologians and Platonists reign deep within the labyrinth. Each man who goes into it increases their number. For every one of them is misled into believing that everything outside the

101 Cf. previous footnote.

102 *Piscator hominum*. In the *Vulgate*, the Latin
     translation of the Bible probably used by Floria,
     Mark 1, 17, reads: *Ex dixit eis Iesus venite post me et
     faciam vos fieri piscatores hominum*. Cf. Matthew 4,
     19.

103 Conf. X, 30. I have speculated over whether
     Floria's simile was written as a conscious attempt
     to formulate a contrast to Plato's cave simile,
     which she would most probably have known.

104 *Omnem crede diem tibi diluxisse supremum*.

labyrinth is the devil's work. Now it is your turn to be misled, and soon you stop wanting to get out of the labyrinth. That is because you too have joined the theologians' band, now you too have become one of those devourers of men in the depths of the dark labyrinth.[101] Or perhaps I should say a fisher of men?[102] You don't forget the woman you loved, but you praise God that now you are separated from her. For now she can no longer tempt you. Only in your dreams 'images of things that were fixed by old habit live on'.[103]

May God forgive you. Perhaps he is somewhere watching you scorn all his works. So many times in your confessions you write that in your earlier life you were where God is not. But suppose it is only now that you are on the wrong road? Oedipus also believed he was on the right road when he travelled from Delphi to Thebes. That was *his* tragic mistake. Everything would have been much better if he had gone home to his foster parents in Corinth instead. Much better, Aurel, if you had found your way back to Carthage. Here we can still glimpse God's love in flowers and trees – and in Venus, Aurel.

I would remind you of some words from Horace: 'Always believe that each day that dawns is your last'.[104] Of course it isn't certain that this is your last day, but it may well turn out to be. Seen thus it might also be thought there is no life for our souls after this one. It could be so, old rhetor, and now I want you to consider this possibility once again. To think that the Bishop of Hippo may have made an error!

Life is short, it is all too short. But perhaps it is here

105 Conf. VI, 16, 'with you', i.e. with God.

106 See footnote 100.

107 Conf. VII, 1.

108 Ibid.

109 *Frondem in silvis non cernis?* Roughly approximates
     to: 'Can't you see the wood for the trees?'

and now that we live, and only here and now. If that is so, haven't you then turned your back on those days that in spite of everything shine – and lost your way in a dark and gloomy labyrinth of ideas where I cannot reach you and lead you out again?

We don't live for ever, Aurel. That does not mean that we shouldn't seize the days we are given.

About your soul – which you love above everything – you write towards the end of your Book Six: 'Wherever it turned, on its back, on its side, or on its stomach, everywhere was *hard*. With you alone is rest.'[105]

I'm led to think again of all the days and nights we spent together in Carthage. We found a deep rest in each other as well. It was then you said: 'Where you are, I want to be.' But you didn't keep that promise. Like a thief you tore yourself away from me and slunk into the maze of theology without taking my guiding thread with you.[106]

You start Book Seven with these words: 'By now my wicked and sinful youth was at an end, and I embarked on the years of manhood. But the older I became the more reason I had to be ashamed of my barrenness.'[107] Although what is sin, your Grace? And what is wickedness? Or barrenness? Isn't it everything that divides us from God?

You continue: 'I could imagine no other reality than that which we normally see with our two eyes.'[108] But now imagine there is no other reality! Then you haven't turned towards the light, but away from it!

Can't you see the leaves on the trees, Aurel?[109] Can

you still see that there is a world around you? If what you see with the naked eye doesn't please you, you could blind yourself. Although that to me would be the same as blasphemy.

You write further that gradually you understood clearly and knew with certainty 'that which is perishable is inferior to what is imperishable'.[110] This sounds acceptably wise and considered, I admit. Although the question is whether, taking everything into account, there *is* such a thing as 'the imperishable' for our souls to cling to. And if there isn't anything imperishable to catch hold of, then in my opinion it is sillier to search for the imperishable than it is to seek the perishable. Now, I assume that your eyes have not yet been gouged out and for that matter that the Bishop of Hippo hasn't castrated himself for the sake of the kingdom of heaven. Poetic enthusiasm, Aurel. Can you forgive?

You go on in this vein to record what you have seen with your inner eye and your love for that which has no body. I shudder. Imagine finding someone who had the power of silencing birdsong merely because they had heard a still more beautiful song with their inner ear? Or imagine someone with the power of making every flower and tree wither because they had smelled a still better perfume than nature's own scents with their inner nose? Indeed, imagine someone who had the power to smash every house and every object of art in the whole world because they had invested all their love in incoporeal things?

For me the birds ceased to sing. The flowers were not

as colourful as before, no one smelled my hair. And no one embraced my body. So I did share some of Dido's fate after all. But I shall not let go of the cameo I hold in my hand.

VIII

111   See 1, Corinthians 13, 12. In the *Vulgate*
      translation: *Videmus nunc per speculum in enigmate,*
      tunc autem facie ad faciem, nunc cognosco ex parte, tunc
      autem cognoscam sicut et cognitus sum. (For now we
      see through a glass, darkly, now face to face: now
      I know in part; but then shall I know even as also
      I am known. *Authorised Version.*)

112   Conf. VIII, 1.

113   Ibid.

114   Ibid.

IN BOOK EIGHT you describe your own conversion in Milan, for after all you did find a kind of peace. You write: 'By then I was convinced of eternal life in you, even if I only saw it as through a glass darkly.[111] But I had been released from all doubts about the existence of an imperishable being from whom all other beings originate.'[112]

All right, dear Aurel, it may be that an imperishable being who has created the whole world and all other living creatures on earth, women and children included, does exist. What remain a puzzle to me are the conclusions you draw from your belief.

'I was displeased with myself for leading a worldly life,' you write. 'It was like a heavy burden weighing me down.'[113] And you elaborate on what you mean by a worldly life: 'I was still firmly bound to the love of woman. The apostle did not forbid me to marry; but he exhorted me to something better, and would far prefer all men to emulate him. But weak as I was, I chose the standpoint where I felt most at ease. That alone was to blame for my lurching listlessly hither and thither in other ways as well. I grew ill, preyed on by consuming worries.'[114]

A little later you add: 'Thus there were two wills in me

115   Conf. VIII, 5.

116   Ibid.

in conflict with one another, an old will and a new, one carnal and the other spiritual. And through this strife they caused a split in my mind.'[115]

It must have been at this time you wrote me a letter, where you also speak out about how sorely you miss our embraces. But you must not let this letter worry you, I shall not show it to the priest.

Your confessions continue: 'Thus I was pleasantly held down by the burden of this world, rather as when one is asleep. And the thoughts of you I struggled with resembled the efforts people make when they are trying to wake up but are overwhelmed by fatigue and sink back into deep sleep. Naturally, no one wants to be asleep constantly. Any sane person thinks it best to be awake. All the same, when our limbs are heavy and relaxed, we often delay shaking off slumber and prefer to stay asleep, even though we don't really enjoy it and even though it's time to get up. Likewise, I was sure it was better to give myself over to your love than to give in to my passions.'[116]

Now, really, Aurel! Are you going to say it yet again? I think you're repeating yourself now, not so untypically in fact, you could harp on constantly about the same thing time and again! And you just go on and on again now: 'Many years of my life had passed – about twelve – since at the age of nineteen I read Cicero's *Hortensius* and the desire for wisdom awakened in me. But I put off despising earthly happiness and devoting myself to the search for true happiness. Not merely finding it but the very seeking of it is preferable to having found all the

117   Conf. VIII, 7.

118   Conf. VIII, 7 and VIII, 10.

119   Conf. VIII, 11.

world's treasures and kingdoms and to physical joys, even though they might be floating around at one's disposal.'[117]

You go on to write of how God released you from the chains of sensual lust. 'Give me purity and abstinence, but not yet!' you prayed. 'For I was afraid you would grant my prayers at once, and heal me of the disease of sensual lust immediately. But I preferred to have it satisfied rather than make an end to it ... I was not totally willing, yet not totally unwilling.'[118]

Then eventually your new bride came and embraced you, 'fair and cheerful, but not frivolous in her joy'.[119]

I am almost moved to congratulate you, for in one way you did in fact get married, to an invisible queen it is true, but she was after all the one you desired. In that way too you could marry without being obliged to bring some new woman into your mother's house. So she gained the upper hand, she must have been highly pleased, you don't try to hide that. She had you both married and baptised at one and the same time.

You write of your violent emotions after your conversion – I was about to say wedding: 'Then a great storm broke out, bringing with it a huge flood of tears. To give them rein to pour out freely I rose and walked away from Alypius. If I had to weep I felt it more suitable to be alone. I went far enough away so as not to be embarrassed by his presence. That was how I felt then, and he realised it. I think I had said something or other that caused my voice to reveal I was on the point of weeping. And so I rose. Alypius stayed where he was, in

120 Conf. VIII, 12.

121 *Omnia vicerant amorem.* I imagine Floria has turned
     Vergil's 'love conquers all' on its head here. For in
     Vergil as well the word order is *omnia vincit amor.*
     Aeneas, incidentally, was the son of Aphrodite,
     goddess of love (Venus).

122 Conf. VIII, 12.

great amazement. Without being aware of it I threw myself down beneath a fig tree and let the tears run freely. They poured streaming from my eyes like a pleasing sacrifice to you.'[120]

So you sought shelter again beneath a fig tree, and in a way that closed the circle, for you must have thought of our fig tree here at home in Carthage. 'Have you been to Rome?' you asked. A cold shudder runs down my back when I think of that, for in the light of your confessions, what happened at that time becomes almost prophetic. Can it be that any of those tears that streamed from your eyes were for me as well?

Not until you collapsed under a fig tree in Milan had Aeneas found his promised land. Now it was perfected: Everything had conquered love![121]

You write: 'Then we go to my mother. We tell her what has happened. Oh, how she rejoices! ... For you had converted me to yourself so that now I neither wished for a wife nor anything else on which we put our faith in this world. Now I stood on that treetrunk of faith where you had brought her to see me in a vision many years earlier. You turned her sorrow to joy, a joy far richer than that she had wished for, and much more precious and pure than what she had once expected to get by having a grandchild through me.'[122]

All the same, weren't you too quick to write off Adeodatus's potential in this sphere? At that point you could not know anything about his unhappy fate. Or did the poor boy allow himself to be embraced by Abstinence as well? Or did you no longer consider him as your

123   Conf. IX, 6.

124   Ibid.

son? Oh, well, he was a bastard, of course, and we have not yet reached the last act of the tragedy.

About the return journey to Verecundus from the country estate you write in Book Nine: 'We took with us Adeodatus, my natural son, the fruit of my sin. You had endowed him well. He was about fifteen years old, but his intelligence surpassed that of many worthy and learned men. I praise you for your gifts, Lord my God, you who created all things and have the power to turn our vileness into something beautiful. For I had no other part in that lad than the sin. And the discipline we raised him with from early childhood was due solely to your encouragement. I praise you for your gifts.'[123]

You go on to write: 'There is a book I wrote entitled *The Teacher*. It is a conversation between him and me. You know that all thoughts expressed through the mouth of the person conversing with me are real thoughts Adeodatus had in his sixteenth year. I heard many other things too from him that were more remarkable. I trembled with awe at his intelligence. And who else but you can perform such marvels? You took him early from this life here on earth. So I can think of him all the more confidently without anxiety for his childhood or youth or the whole of his life.'[124]

I make no secret of the intense pain it causes me to read these lines. I tremble too, but for another reason. I don't know whether it was God who took Adeodatus away from life here on earth, I have no opinion to give on that. I know only that it was you who took him away from his mother. Adeodatus was my only child, your

125 The expression 'hen-pecked' (*tøffelhelt*: 'slipper
hero' in Norwegian) existed as far back as late
antiquity. However, I have been unable to find
any occurrence of the word either in dictionaries
or in any text from late antiquity. Here Floria uses
the word *crepundia* which should probably be
translated as 'rattle' (a child's toy) or 'bangles' or
'baubles', from *crepo*, rattle, jangle or clatter. But cf.
also *crepida*, Greek sandal, a derivative of the same
verb! Directly translated, then, Floria describes
Aurel as Abstinence's 'bauble'. I have chosen a
freer translation, the Norwegian 'slipper hero', for
Floria's *crepundia*. [I have rendered the Norwegian
as English 'hen-pecked': Translator.]

Grace! Was it not in your care that he finally faded away and died, leaving us both?

How happy you must be now that you don't have to worry because Adeodatus too might have been lured beneath a fig tree by a capricious woman. I myself would have been more worried in case he might one day fall to his knees before Abstinence – as her slave and henpecked husband.[125]

IX

Now I follow you by saying I'm leaving out a great deal to get to what is essential to me more quickly. Besides, I have used half my fortune on parchment and haven't many sheets left to write on.

On your way back to Africa you arrived at Ostia on the Tiber. There you and Monica had a 'wonderful conversation' in which you sought 'to discover the nature of the eternal life in which the saints shall participate'. The conversation led you to 'the result that the greatest pleasure the bodily senses can give, in the most radiant earthly glory, is by comparison with the joy of eternity not even worthy of comparison, let alone mention.'[126]

You must forgive me, your Grace, but I am a cultivated woman now. So in all humility I feel a certain need to suggest that this sounds like a kind of conjuration. For what if you should be wrong on precisely this decisive point? Then you would have given the prize to Epicure, you said when we were still together. I myself believe that you and Adeodatus would have come back to Carthage at once. For then you would have had no choice, then you would have had to live as a whole human being here and now, and I think you would have

127 Conf. IX, 11.

had more than enough of earthly love to share with both me and others.

Life is so short we do not have time to pronounce any damning judgement on love. We must first live, Aurel, then we can philosophise.

But we must on no account forget Monica. For it was in Ostia that she fell ill with a fever. And you had learned that 'with motherly confidence' she had talked to some of your friends 'about despising this life, and about how good it is to die'.[127] Sic!

She was a pious person – who managed to despise this life, I mean. However, I feel the need to add that that might be the same as despising God's work of creation. For we do not know if God has created any other world for us. I realise I am starting to repeat myself, but that may well be because you repeat yourself just as much in your confessions, your Grace. I am of the opinion that it must be human arrogance to reject this life – with all its earthly joys – in favour of an existence which is perhaps merely an abstraction. Surely you haven't forgotten Aristoteles's criticism of all such ideas of an ideal world?

Life is so short, Aurel. We are free to hope for a life after this one. But we are not free to treat each other and ourselves badly, almost like an instrument with which to attain an existence we know nothing about. Besides, there is another possibility to which you give absolutely no consideration in any of your books. As imperial rhetor you should at least have discussed the possibility of there being an eternal life for individual souls, but that the grounds of judgement are different from those you

128 Ibid.

129 Conf. IX, 12.

yourself almost take for granted. For instance, I believe it is not necessarily a greater sin to engage in physical love with the woman in one's life than it is to separate that same woman from her only son. I myself take pleasure in the idea that the God who created heaven and earth is the same God who created Venus. Do you remember when I was with child? Or when I nurtured little Adeodatus at my breast? Even then you dared to hold me, and you sought no other.

Was that the time when you were furthest away from God?

I'm not saying I know any of this. I'm only saying I don't know. I'm not even saying that I don't believe in God's judgement. I'm only saying that I may also believe in the judgement of turning one's back on all the joys, all the warmth and all the tenderness that the Bishop of Hippo Regius now denies. This is Floria's confession!

Then Monica died on the ninth day of her illness, in her fifty-sixth year, and in my thirty-third, Aurel. Then 'this devout and pious soul was released from the body'.[128] You write: 'When she had drawn her last breath, my boy Adeodatus began to weep loudly with sorrow.' But you 'felt it was not seemly to grieve for the dead with tears and moans. For that may be suitable where the dead are mourned because of their miserable lot or because their death is seen as complete annihilation. But death was no misfortune for Mother. In fact, it was no death.'[129]

Peace be to her memory, Bishop! You do not conceal the fact that you too felt pain, bitter pain, and as soon as

130 Cf. the Greek word *hybris* – which was met with the gods' wrath (*nemesis*). Floria uses the Latin word *superbia* here.

131 *Te hominem esse memento*. These words were to be whispered in the ear of a victor during his triumphal procession through Rome.

132 Cf. Cicero in his first speech to Catilina: How long, Catilina, will you misuse our patience?

133 Monica's grave in Ostia was found in the summer of 1945 in front of the church of Santa Aurea by two boys digging a hole for a basketball goalpost.

134 *Fit erranti medicina confessio.*

you were alone you allowed the tears to flow freely. It is true that you are slightly ashamed of weeping tears over your mother, for that could be seen as a sign that you still nourished earthly feelings.

Do you remember we once talked of the arrogance of the Greek heroes?[130] I think it isn't out of place here to remind you that you too are merely human.[131] For how long, Aurel, will you try my patience?[132] No matter how much you squirm, you too have 'earthly feelings', if you have any feelings at all, I mean, for what other feelings would those you especially possess be?

Then I received the second letter from my Aurel ...

After Monica was buried at Ostia,[133] you went to Rome with Adeodatus, and both of you stayed there for almost a whole year. But you do not write anything about this year in your confessions, your Grace. Why not? Is there after all a limit to your need to confess?

To confess is medicine for one who has gone astray, writes Cicero.[134] But you do not confess to your gravest faults! How can you just cross out the last act of the tragedy? For what can we learn from the tragedy if we delete *that*?

After Monica died you must have been suddenly cast out into a state of doubt and emptiness. For now you were left alone with a son, Monica was gone, and you missed me, Aurel, you missed me. So also must Adeodatus have done, it was two years since he had seen me. But he was never to see me more, and I never saw him again.

You wrote in your letter that Monica was dead, and I

135   *Video meliora proboque, deteriora sequor.* Cf. St Paul,
      Romans, 7, 19. In the *Vulgate: Non enim quod volo
      bonum hoc facio sed quod nolo malum hoc ago.*

shall not plague you by quoting everything here
now, but you were eager to tell me that the engagen
had long since been annulled, and that you would never
marry. But you might need to be reminded of your
concluding greetings. You write: 'How I miss you,
Floria! I wish you could have been with us now. I want
to see you, I both want to see you and at the same time I
don't want to. I want to, but I cannot, and I cannot, but I
would.'

It can then sometimes be hard for a person to make a
decision, and is it so strange that sometimes it goes
wrong? 'I know what is good for me, but do what is
harmful to me,' writes Ovid.[135]

It was then you allowed Adeodatus to add a few words
to his mother. So sweet of you, Aurel, and so thoughtful,
for he must have felt such pleasure now that a couple of
years had passed since he and I had last seen each other.

It was a mutual loss, and I interpreted your words to
mean you wanted to see me. So I journeyed to Rome. I
was lucky and obtained a passage in just a few days.

There was one sentence that seemed to fret my ears
the whole time: 'Have you been to Rome?' When I
arrived there for the second time, and this time quite
alone, I had to go round the congregations to ask my
way. But after only a few days we met each other up on
the Aventine, and we were able to put our arms around
each other again.

We stayed a long time like that, looking deep into
each other's eyes, as deep as our gaze could reach. Didn't
it seem in that hour that we were one single living soul

that somehow reflected itself in itself? Then there was something you said, Aurel, can you remember? Now you must be with me always, you said!

You did not *fall* when for a few short weeks we resumed our old life together. I mean you rose up to new life after having lived in the theologians' valley of shadows. So what happened during those weeks holds nothing to confess either to God or men. I hope it is out of regard for what happened later that you write nothing about that time in your books.

Do you remember when we were down in the Forum looking up at the snow that had fallen on the imperial palaces? You saw I was cold, but then you drew me close, so close I could feel how your blood grew warm. I remember I turned to you and said you had no shame. But I wanted it too. We were two people, although we had only one desire.

We couldn't live under the same roof, for you didn't want Adeodatus to meet me, not to begin with, at least, you said. I could have died with longing to see him. But you thought he would be so disappointed if anything should happen after all to prevent the great reunion. So you rented this room up on the Aventine, a place where only you and I could see each other.

How can we forget that winter, Aurel? Again we were both in Venus's court with the freedom to play in her arms. Didn't you say then that you felt like a withered tree which suddenly rises again because rain has fallen after a long dry summer?

It is not merely to shield you that I keep this brief.

One afternoon you turned to me in a sudden rage, it was after we had shared the gifts of Venus again. Then you hit me. Do you remember how you hit me? You, Aurel, you who were once a respected teacher of rhetoric, you beat me almost senseless because you had allowed yourself to be tempted by my tenderness. So it was I who had to bear the blame for your lust. I have already cited Horace, but I will gladly do so again: When foolish people want to avoid making a mistake, they usually do the opposite thing!

You hit me and screamed, Bishop, because now I posed a threat again to the salvation of your soul. Then you seized a stick and beat me again. I wondered if you might want to beat the life out of me, for that might certainly serve the same purpose as if you had castrated yourself. I was not so afraid for my own skin, I was just so broken, so disappointed and so ashamed of my Aurel that I clearly and distinctly remember wishing that you would do away with me now once and for all.

Suddenly I had become something you could not just turn your back on for the sake of your soul's salvation. I myself had become the bleeding sacrificial lamb that was necessary to open the gates of heaven.

Then you wept, I shall not forget that. You had stopped beating me, but I had several bleeding wounds. And you wept, and you comforted me, and you begged me for forgiveness. Everything was so different now Monica was no longer here, you explained.

You folded your hands and begged, now me, now your God, for pardon. You found some cloth and bound

up my wounds. I myself was merely cold and frightened, cold because I was still bleeding, and frightened because I had seen right into a kind of wickedness I had had no inkling of.

It was as if something completely new had begun, a new time. The old time, that came to an end when we two crossed the River Arno together. Then followed several years of great confusion and doubt. Then the new time began when you suddenly hit me. I thought only one thought: 'You, Aurel! You!'

You sent me back to Carthage. I heard no more from you before Adeodatus died two years later.

X

136 In the classical period, performances of the Greek
     tragedies were followed by so-called satyr plays.
     The satyrs were lively, riotous and half-divine
     beings characterised as goat-like creatures in human
     form. I see a weighty dose of irony in Floria's
     description of Augustine's Book Ten as a satyr
     play, in particular perhaps indicating the idea that a
     (half-divine) bishop continues to bemoan his lustful
     urges and needs to his dying day.

137 Conf. X, 31.

THE TRAGEDY IS ended, Bishop. There remains only the satyr play.[136] For I have also copied some extracts from your Book Ten.

I have mentioned several times already how you deal with sense after sense and passion after passion as you praise the Lord because you have hardly any earthly feelings any more. Although it is a little difficult for you to regulate your daily intake of food so that it is precisely sufficient to maintain health but no more. So you wage 'a daily war, often in fasting' as you keep your 'body in bondage'. You write: 'For this is not something I can decide to give up once and for all and never return to, as I was able to do with sexual intercourse.'[137]

And there we are again, for it was there I wanted to go. You write: 'You have forbidden relations outside marriage. And even if you allow marriage, you have encouraged us to take up something better. And because you gave me abstinence, this took place even before I became a minister of your sacrament. But in my memory, which I have spoken of so much, there still live images of acts firmly imprinted from old habit. They force themselves upon me, albeit not strongly when I am awake; but in sleep they tempt me, not only to pleasure but to assent and act upon them. These ensnaring images

138 Conf. X, 30.

139 Presumably Floria plays on Achilles's words on the
     shadow life of the kingdom of death: 'I would
     rather be above ground still and labouring for
     some poor portionless man, than be lord over all
     the lifeless dead' Homer, *The Odyssey* (Walter
     Shewring's translation, *World's Classics*, OUP).
     Thus Floria makes Augustine one of the living
     dead – in the Church's kingdom of death – as he
     himself countless times compares a life in 'sensual
     passion' with death.

140 Conf. X, 30.

141 *Multa petentibus desunt multa.*

142 A play on the saying *Lupus pilum mutat, non
     mentem.*

have such power over my soul and body that what I imagine I see in sleep persuades me to give way to actions which nothing I see in reality when I am awake can make me succumb to. Lord, my God, I am not myself then, am I?'[138]

No, Aurel, perhaps you are only a shadow of yourself. It would probably have been better if you were a poor slave on earth than a high priest in the theologians' gloomy labyrinth.[139]

Once more you will pray to your God for help in such questions: 'Is not your mercy more than generous enough to eradicate the impure passions that still possess me even in sleep? Indeed, Lord, you will let your gifts of grace increase more and more in me, so my soul – released from the snares of lust – can accompany me to you. Then it will no longer be at war with itself, and will not, owing to sensual images, force the body into such shameful indecency in sleep as to give vent to sinful emissions, nay, it will not even want them. You can cause it not to desire that kind of thing ...'[140]

Poor Aurel! He who desires much, lacks much, writes Horace.[141] For you are almost fifty already, I am tempted to say I am impressed. Besides, I feel quite proud to have made such an indelible impression on you. On that spring day in Carthage when you came and sat down beneath the fig tree with me I had no presentiment that our love would be so tempestuous. But 'bodily passions' cannot be obliterated by abstinence, this much I now realise. For the wolf only changes its skin, your Grace, it does not change its nature![142] Or as Zenon would have

143 Zeno of Elea, Greek philosopher of about 460 BC, known for his proofs of the impossibility of diversity and movement, e.g. the paradox of Achilles and the tortoise. However, the play here is on a quotation not documented in any existing source. Most probably it is Floria's memory that is at fault here.

144 Conf. X, 33.

145 Ibid.

put it: Why should it be so hard to run away from one's own shadow?[143]

So if we enjoy the taste of food or love, we must know how to steer away from both. You also write that you are ready to dispense with the temptations of the sense of smell for ever. I have asked myself what will be left in the end, your Grace, of our life on earth, I mean. For hearing too offers its perilous temptations, you know. You write: 'The joys hearing can give us had taken a firm hold on me and forced me to bow under its yoke. But you have released me and liberated me. I admit that I still find satisfaction in the melodies to which your words give life and soul when they are sung artistically by a fine voice … So I sin in this without noticing; but afterwards I feel it is sin.'[144] Sometimes you could wish that all the wonderful melodies to which the Psalms of David are sung were removed, not only from your ears but from those of the whole church, you write. And you go on: 'I think, then, that Bishop Athanasius of Alexandria managed things more satisfactorily, according to what I often recall having heard about him: he had the cantor sing the psalm with so little variation in the pitch that it resembled speech rather than song.'[145] Unfortunate congregation, your Grace. Should not art be a divine service? And shouldn't divine service also be an art?

You have stopped loving, Aurel. As you have also stopped enjoying food, stopped smelling the flowers, and you have stopped listening too much to psalm singing. Then you write: 'Now I have yet to speak again of the sensual lust of my eyes … The eyes love beautiful

146 Conf. X, 34.

147 See footnote 40.

148 Conf. X, 35.

149 *Si tacuisses, philosophus mansisses.* (If you had only
   kept quiet, one would have gone on believing you
   were wise.) In my view this is Floria's most
   remarkable formulation. The expression is known
   from *The Consolations of Philosophy* by Boethius (c.
   480–524) – i.e. about a hundred years after Floria's
   letter. For me this is a powerful indication that
   Boethius – directly or indirectly – must have
   known Floria's letter, at least in part. Boethius was
   very familiar with Augustine's writings. It is surely
   not improbable that he was also familiar with the
   Codex Floria. At least a few adages from Floria's
   letter may have reached him.

changing forms and brilliant, fine colours. But this shall not possess my soul. That is for God to have. It is true that he created everything exceedingly well, but he, not the creation, is my good.' Then it is as if you give a deep sigh as you say that physical light 'has an alluring perilous sweetness, which enhances life for those who love this world blindly'. And you continue thus: 'So inestimably much human beings have done to augment the temptations of the eyes, through various types of art and craft: with clothes and shoes, cups and vessels of all kinds, with paintings and different kinds of art. And in this they more than exceed what is a necessary and reasonable need and what holds religious value. Indeed, outwardly they chase after what they create, and inwardly they desert him who created them, and thus annihilate their distinctive quality as created beings.'[146] I wonder if it is not precisely our quality as created beings to rejoice in God's work of creation, your Grace. Again I want to remind you that it is never too late to follow the example of King Oedipus.[147]

You seem to round the whole thing off by warning against the temptations invited by human curiosity: 'It does not wish to take its pleasure in the flesh, but with the aid of the flesh it wants to gain experience, through the same bodily senses. And so it decks itself out with names like understanding and knowledge. This desire is an urge for knowledge ...'[148] This is how you write, Aurel, you who were once appointed to the post of imperial rhetor in Milan. If only you had kept quiet you could have gone on passing yourself off as a philosopher![149]

150   Conf. X, 35.

151   From Greek mythology: Dedalus made wings out
      of birds' feathers and beeswax so that he and his
      son Icarus could fly and so escape from Crete.
      Dedalus warned Icarus not to fly too near the sun,
      which would melt the wax. But the arrogant
      Icarus disregarded his father's warning and flew so
      close to the sun that it burned off his wings and
      Icarus crashed into the sea.

152   *Epistula non erubescit*, Cicero.

153   Floria writes 'look up at Jupiter', that is, Father
      Jove, the god of heaven. Thus 'Under heaven' can
      stand for *sub Iove* (under Jove), for instance in
      Horace.

Moreover, you warn against allowing the mind to be captivated by the course of the stars – or by a dog running after a hare. And you deal with the question in a concrete way as if to elaborate on how natural it is to fall for the temptation to be diverted by what the eyes see. You write: 'Often when I sit at home I eagerly watch a lizard catching flies, or the spider which spins its thread around them when it entraps them in its net. Insignificant creatures, to be sure. But doesn't it come to the same thing? From such sights I turn to praising you, who in a wonderful way create and order all things. But it was not that which captured my attention from the start. One thing is to rise swiftly, another is not to fall at all.'[150]

I myself come to think of Icarus.[151] At first he rose swiftly, but then he fell plop. It was because he had forgotten that he was only a human being. If you think there is a better comparison, I could also remind you of what happened to the people of Babylon after they had tried to build a tower so high that it reached right into heaven.

I write as sincerely as you, your Grace, and the letter will not blush.[152] I think you must be exhausted after all you have been through, really exhausted, you do not hide the fact, either. If only you could give me now – and thus the physical world – a few hours more of your life on earth. Go out, Aurel! Go out and lie down beneath a fig tree. Open your senses – if only for this very last time. For my sake, Aurel, and for everything we two once gave each other. Draw breath, listen to birdsong, look up at the vault of the sky[153] and draw all

154 Floria plays on some words by Plautus: *Oleum et operam perdidi* (I have spilt my oil and my efforts). The words are ascribed to a girl who has tried in vain to be a success with the other sex.

the odours to yourself. It is this that is the world, Aurel, and it is here now. Here, now. You have been into the labyrinth of the theologians and the Platonists. But no longer, now you have come back to the world again, to our human home.

The world is so big, and we know far too little about it. And life is far too short. Do you remember you could say something similar when you read Cicero?

Perhaps there is no God who bargains with our poor souls. Or perhaps there is a loving God, who has created us for the world so that we shall live here. Oh, Aurel, if you were lying out there beneath a fig tree – I think you're holding a fig in one hand – then I should surely come and kiss you on your all too worn brow. I would try to chew up that fearfully wearing word 'abstinence'. For still, yes still, that word lies like a heavy burden on your mind. The only thing that might possibly have released you would have been my embrace. Why does Carthage have to be so far from Hippo Regius?

I shall see to it that you receive this letter, so I will beg you to read it. But I no longer hold out any hope that the words I write will truly reach you. Thus I have spilt my oil and my efforts.[154]

I am beset with fear, Aurel. I am afraid of what the men of the church may one day do to women like me. Not just because we are women – as God has created us women. But because we tempt you who are men – as God has created you men. You think God loves eunuchs and castrati above those men who love a woman. Then

155   Cf. Syrus: *Multis minatur, qui uni facit iniuriam.*

be cautious how you praise God's work of creation, for God did not create man to castrate himself.

I cannot forget what happened in Rome, and I no longer think of myself. For really it was not I upon whom you unleashed your rage that day. It was Eve, your Grace, the woman. And he who wrongs one, threatens many.[155]

I shiver, for I fear the day will come when women like me will be done away with by the men of the universal church. And why will they be done away with, your Grace? Because they remind you that you have denied your own soul and gifts. And for whom? For a God, you all say, for him who created a heaven above you and also an earth which actually holds women who bring you into the world.

If God exists, may he forgive you. But perhaps you will be judged one day for all the joys of life you have turned your backs on. You renounce the love between man and woman. It may perhaps be forgiven. But you do it in the name of God.

Life is short, and we know far too little. But if it was at your behest that your confessions were given me to read here in Carthage, the answer is no. I shall not allow myself to be baptised, your Grace. It is not God I fear. I feel that I live with him already, and was it not he who created me, after all? Nor is it the Nazarene who holds me back, he probably really was a man of God. And was he not also fair to women? It is the theologians I fear. May the God of the Nazarene forgive you for all the tenderness and all the love you proscribed.

156 *Dixi et salvavi animam meam.*

157 *Nunc est bibendum*, Horace.

158 *Floret* (from *floreo*, to bloom, flower). I would
     think Floria is again playing on her own name.
     For that matter, the name *Floria* must have derived
     from *flos, floris* (flower). Cf. *Flora*, goddess of
     flowers.
         A mile or two beyond Ostia the ruins of an old
     Augustinian monastery lie today (San Agostino).
     The monastery was built in the Middle Ages on
     the bank of the River Fiora (Floria) where it runs
     into the sea. In my opinion this is surely a sign
     that a Floria tradition must have existed some way
     into the medieval period.

159 *Fructum, av fructus*, which can also mean 'use',
     'reward' or 'profit'. But Floria has also read the
     four gospels. Can she have had the parable of the
     fig tree in mind? (See Matthew 21, 18–22, and
     Luke 13, 6–9).

160 *Vale!* Conventional leave-taking expression in
     letters.

I have spoken and I have unleashed my soul.[156] And now, your Grace, now is the time for drinking![157] I am sitting beneath our old fig tree in Carthage. It is blooming[158] for the third time this year. But it bears no fruit.[159]

Farewell![160]

I AM LEFT *with many questions. Did Floria send her letter to Aurel? Or when it came to the point didn't she have the courage? There is a suggestion of that in the letter. She writes that she is afraid of what the men of the church might one day do to a woman like her.*

As some of the footnotes indicate, I feel fairly convinced that the letter really was sent to the Bishop of Hippo Regius. One possibility is that the letter has lived a more or less hidden life throughout the history of the Roman Catholic Church. Even if it may have been handed down in several copies, the letter need not have been known to many people. And naturally the original parchment may also – intentionally or unintentionally – have remained concealed until it suddenly turned up in the sixteenth century. But what happened after that?

Perhaps my copy of the 'Codex Floriae' lay in a monastery library until it was recently found and then sold to the little antiquarian bookshop in Buenos Aires. The proprietor said something about protecting his clients. Even a priest – or a nun for that matter – can find themselves in circumstances leading to pecuniary necessity.

As regards the actual delivery of the letter I can visualise another possibility. Whether Augustine received it from Floria or not, perhaps the old parchment was found by the Arabs when they invaded North Africa in the seventh century. They may then have taken it with them to Spain, where it was preserved for many centuries before being rediscovered and taken to South America by the Spanish conquerors.

Does the old parchment still exist?

I am, however, more interested in another question: how did Augustine react to the letter from his one-time lover? What did he do with it? And what did he do about Floria?

It is unlikely that we shall ever know for certain whether Augustine received Floria's letter. Although as late as a few years ago a previously unknown Augustine letter was found (Peter Brown, The Body and Society, *Columbia University Press, N.Y., 1988, p. 397).*

And indeed, it was incredibly naive of me not to ask the Vatican Library for a receipt at least!

Jostein Gaarder
Oslo, 8 August 1996

All Orion/Phoenix titles are available at your local bookshop or from the following address:

Littlehampton Book Services
Cash Sales Department L
14 Eldon Way, Lineside Industrial Estate
Littlehampton
West Sussex BN17 7HE
telephone 01903 721596, *facsimile* 01903 730914

Payment can either be made by credit card (Visa and Mastercard accepted) or by sending a cheque or postal order made payable to *Littlehampton Book Services*.
DO NOT SEND CASH OR CURRENCY.

Please add the following to cover postage and packing

UK and BFPO:
£1.50 for the first book, and 50P for each additional book to a maximum of £3.50

Overseas and Eire:
£2.50 for the first book plus £1.00 for the second book and 50p for each additional book ordered

----

BLOCK CAPITALS PLEASE

name of cardholder ....   *delivery address*
                             ....   *(if different from cardholder)*
address of cardholder ....

....

....

....
        postcode ....   *postcode* ....

☐   I enclose my remittance for   £..............................

☐   please debit my Mastercard/Visa (delete as appropriate)

card number ☐☐☐☐☐☐☐☐☐☐☐☐☐☐☐☐

expiry date ☐☐☐☐

signature ....

prices and availability are subject to change without notice